JP

First published in Great Britain in 2008
by Zero To Ten Limited
2A Portman Mansions, Chiltern Street,
London W1U 6NR

This edition © 2008 Zero To Ten Limited
© Gallimard Jeunesse 2007

First published in France in 2007 as
Le Pique-Nique de Rita et Machin

Translated by Su Swallow

British Library Cataloguing in Publication Data:
Arrou-Vignod, Jean-Philippe, 1958-
Rita and Whatsit go on a picnic
1. Rita (Fictitious character : Arrou-Vignod) - Pictorial
works - Juvenile fiction 2. Whatsit (Fictitious character)
- Pictorial works - Juvenile fiction 3. Picknicking -
Pictorial works - Juvenile fiction 4. Children's stories -
Pictorial works
I. Title II. Tallec, Olivier
843.9'14[J]

ISBN-13: 9781840895261

Printed in China

JEAN-PHILIPPE ARROU-VIGNOD ✱ OLIVIER TALLEC

Rita and Whatsit go on a Picnic

ZERO TO TEN

Rita and Whatsit are going on a picnic.
They're both very excited.
The sun is shining, the car is full of food,
and they're on their way to the countryside.

This is a good spot!
'You'd better behave yourself, Whatsit, or
you'll have to stay in the car!'

Hey, who's opened
the crisps already?
And someone's been
nibbling this salami.

It can't have been Whatsit, can it?
He's busy chasing butterflies.

'Whatsit, look out, you're
treading all over the blanket!
And mind the lemonade!'

Rita and Whatsit, the intrepid explorers, dive
into the long grass.
What could be better than a jungle adventure
before lunch?

Aargh! What's that wild animal?

'Come on Whatsit,
don't be silly. It's only
a cow!'

'I know, let's play hide and seek,' suggests Rita. 'You count while I hide. No peeping, mind.'

Whatsit starts counting. 'One, two, three... 10, 11, 12... 91... 100... I'm coming!'

Rita runs and hides.
Whatsit sets off in pursuit.
There's surely no escape from this cunning
little dog! He'll find Rita in no time!

Won't he?

He creeps up silently and...

...leaps on his prey...
'Whatsit, whatever are you doing?'
cries Rita.
'I'm not a rabbit!'

'Rita! Whatsit! Come and eat!'

There's cold chicken you can eat with your fingers,
sausage rolls, potato salad and strawberries with cream.

It's great being an Indian chief - no cooking, and no washing up!

Then, in the middle of the picnic, the sky turns black, thunder
rumbles, and it starts to pour with rain.
Panic at the picnic.
Quick, into the car!

Bother. Lunch is soggy.
We'll have to go straight home.

Hey, where's Whatsit?
Under the seat? In the
cool box?

Rita starts to worry:
there's no sign of Whatsit in
the car.

'We have to go back, Mum!
We've left Whatsit behind. He'll get
soaked!'

It's raining so hard you can hardly see
the end of your nose.

'Whatsit! Where are you?
Come here now, or I'll cry!'

Rita looks everywhere.
But no luck anywhere.
Rita is worried.
What if a big monster has eaten her friend?

What are those dark shapes over
there under the tree?

'Is that you, you rascal?'
'Hi, Rita,' says Whatsit. 'Let me introduce Penelope,
my new friend.
Isn't she lovely?'

'I don't believe you, Whatsit!' grumbles Rita.
'I was so worried.'

'And you're not even slightly wet!'

Back in the car, the intrepid pair collapse in a heap,
exhausted after their wet adventure.
'You know what, Whatsit?' says Rita. 'Next time we go
on a picnic, we'll make sure to check the weather
forecast first!'

'Talking of food, what about something
to eat?' says Whatsit. 'My stomach's
rumbling.'
Rita is hungry too.

'Let's have a little picnic at home in the dry...
just you and me. Agreed?'